For Jade Surya, our own little trickster
And with thanks to Pak Ledjar for introducing me to Kanchil...

Nathan

Many thanks to Raja Mohanty whose patience, generosity and love
for Patachitra made this project possible.

Tara Publishing

The Sacred Banana Leaf
First published in English by Tara Publishing

Copyright © 2008 Tara Publishing

For the text: Nathan Kumar Scott
For the illustrations: Radhashyam Raut

For this edition:
Tara Publishing Ltd., U.K. <www.tarabooks.com/uk>
and
Tara Publishing, India <www.tarabooks.com>

Design: Avinash Veeraraghavan
Production: C. Arumugam

Printed and bound in Thailand by Sirivatana Interprint PCL

ISBN: 978-81-86211-28-1

The Sacred Banana Leaf

An Indonesian Trickster Tale
Retold by
Nathan Kumar Scott

Art by
Radhashyam Raut

TARA PUBLISHING

It was a nice cool day in the forest.

Kanchil the mouse deer trotted along, quite pleased with himself.

Back from the Sunday market, he was carrying delicious sweet rice cakes wrapped in a big banana leaf.

"The best cakes in the world!" Kanchil sighed happily, taking a big bite. One by one, they disappeared into his mouth. Then Kanchil started licking the banana leaf.

He was so intent on licking every grain of sticky rice off the leaf, that he didn't pay attention to where he was going. And in the forest that can only mean...

CRAAAASH!

One moment Kanchil's feet were on solid ground – and the next moment he was tumbling down... into a deep pit. The banana leaf floated lazily down and settled on top of his head.

Kanchil felt ridiculous!

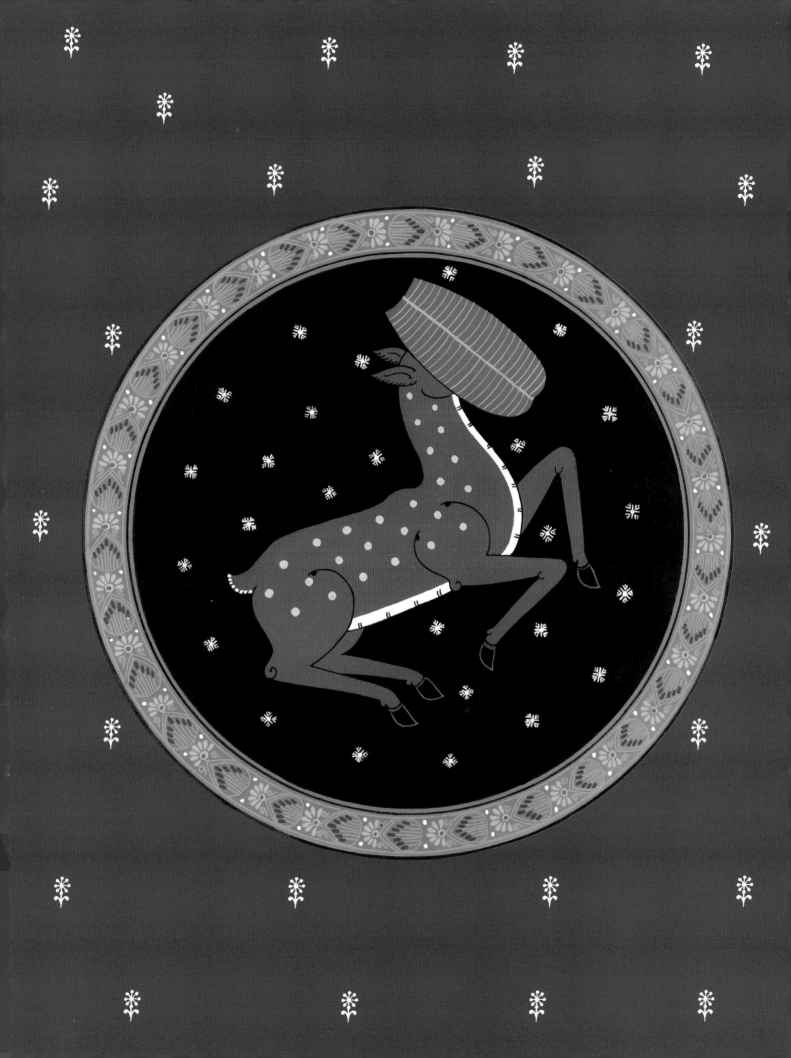

Kanchil tried to find a way out of the pit. He scampered up one side and then another, but it was just too steep and slippery for his little legs to climb.

He tried shouting for help. He shouted and shouted, but nobody heard him. He was stuck at the bottom of the pit! But for how long? Until the end of the world?

THE END OF THE WORLD!!

Suddenly Kanchil had an idea. He would just need to wait.

He didn't have to wait long. Ular the snake soon came slithering along looking for something good to eat.

"Kanchil! What are you doing down there?" Ular wanted to know.

"Haven't you heard?" Kanchil replied, "The world is going to end today! But not for me, because I'm safe here in this pit!"

"How do you know?" Ular asked.

"It says so right here, on this Sacred Banana Leaf I have with me," said Kanchil, pointing to the banana leaf, still sticky from the sweet rice cakes.

"S-s-sacred Banana Leaf?" Ular hissed suspiciously.

"Yes, it's The Eternal Everlasting Sacred Banana Leaf of the Jungle," Kanchil replied. "Here, let me read it for you."

Kanchil peered intently at the leaf:

On this day, in this way

The world shall come to an end

The sky shall fall, upon us all, so be prepared

Only those in the deep pit shall be spared!

"The world coming to an end?! Can I be spared too?" pleaded Ular.

"Well Ular," said Kanchil, "I would let you come down, but my Sacred Banana Leaf says that you can only be in this pit on one condition – NO SNEEZING. Anyone who sneezes must be thrown out. So I'm sorry, you sneeze too much. I can't let you come down."

"I won't sneeze, I won't sneeze! I promise! Can I please come down?" pleaded Ular.

"Oh, all right then. But NO SNEEZING!" warned Kanchil.

So Ular slid down into the pit with Kanchil.

Just then, along came Babi the wild boar, sniffing for food with her powerful nose. She peered into the pit, puzzled.

"What are you doing down there?" Babi asked Kanchil and Ular.

"We're waiting for the end of the world!" replied Kanchil. "According to the Sacred Banana Leaf, the world is going to end today. The sky will fall today, and only those in the pit will be spared."

"The end of the world? Huh! Nonsense! But then again... better safe than sorry! Make way, I'm coming down too!" said Babi.

"No! No, wait!" shouted Kanchil. "We'd be glad to have you, Babi, but the only problem is — you would sneeze. Any animal who sneezes must be thrown out of the pit."

"Well, I won't sneeze, so here I come."

So Babi tumbled into the pit with Kanchil and Ular.
The three of them then waited for the end of the world.

Very soon, Harimau the tiger came sauntering along with a wicked stare.

"What is going on down there?" he roared, when he came to the pit.

"We're waiting for the end of the world! The sky's going to fall today and only those in the pit will be spared. It says so on this Sacred Banana Leaf!"

"The world end today? No forest? No more animals? I'll go hungry!" thought Harimau, always thinking about his stomach. At least in the pit there was a mouse deer, a snake and a wild boar.

"Right! Here I come!" he growled.

"No, no, wait! Harimau! You sneeze too much! Any animal who sneezes has to be thrown out!" said Babi, not happy at all to have a tiger down in the pit with her... for then surely it would be the end of the world!

"I've got to come down! I won't sneeze, I promise!"

So Harimau took a flying leap and landed in the pit.

All of them waited, not sure what the end of the world would look like.

Soon Kanchil looked over at Harimau. "Did I hear you about to sneeze?"

"No, not me!" said Harimau putting his paws over his nose to make sure he didn't sneeze.

Then Kanchil turned to Babi. "Did I hear you about to sneeze?"

"Humpf," replied Babi. "I never sneeze."

Then Kanchil looked straight at Ular. "Were you about to sneeze?"

"Not me! Not me!" cried Ular.

Then, ever so slowly, Kanchil felt his nose begin to twitch. It twitched a little more… and a little more… and a little more. Kanchil tried to stop himself. But it was no use.

Aa… aah… aaah… aaaah… aaaaah… CHOOOOOOOO!!!

Kanchil let out the biggest, loudest, longest sneeze you ever heard!

All the animals stared at Kanchil.

"Kanchil! YOU SNEEZED!" accused Babi.

"It says on your Sacred Banana Leaf that whoever sneezes must be thrown out of the pit!" said Ular.

"So out with you!" declared Harimau.

The three of them took hold of Kanchil by his legs, and saying "One, two, three!" together, threw him out of the pit!

Kanchil found himself on the cool forest floor once more. His plan had worked!

"Thank you!" Kanchil called into the pit. And with that he trotted away as fast as his little legs would take him – quickly, before the others realised what had happened and came charging after him.

All that time in the pit had made Kanchil hungry. So he headed back to the market to look for some more of those delicious sweet rice cakes wrapped in banana leaves.

Kanchil and Trickster Tales Traditions

Nathan Kumar Scott

Trickster tales appear in the folklore of most cultures around the world. They are the popular tales about the wise fool, the clown, or the small animal who outwits the larger and more powerful animals in the jungle. Tricksters and clowns can be human, animal or god-like characters, but their stories always convey social values of the culture they come from.

Kanchil is the popular trickster from Indonesian and Malaysian folklore. He is a tiny deer who lives in the rainforest. Because he is so small, he has to live by his wits in order to survive, or else he would be eaten for lunch by the bigger animals of the forest. Kanchil tales are typically a celebration of brains over brawn, of the victory of the less powerful over those more powerful. But like other tricksters, Kanchil sometimes plays tricks on his friends, and sometimes is tricked by other even smaller animals!

In Indonesia, Kanchil tales are often told through shadow puppetry – called *wayang kancil*. There are many characters in a *wayang kancil* puppet show which goes on for several hours, with Kanchil playing tricks on other animals and having tricks played on him. Both children and adults love these stories and go away after the show to tell their friends about the new adventures of Kanchil they have just learnt.

Can you make up a story about a trick that Kanchil plays on another animal, just like he did in the story of *The Sacred Banana Leaf*?

The Art of Patachitra

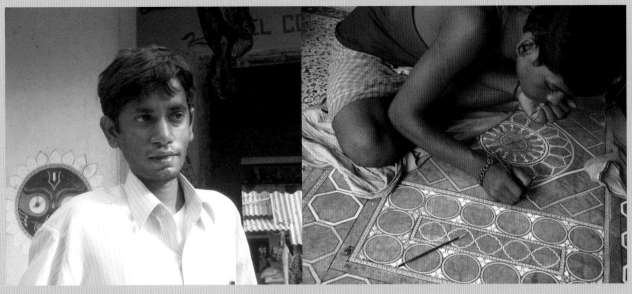

Radhashyam Raut

The art for this story has been especially created by Radhashyam Raut, who is a traditional Indian artist. He paints in the *Patachitra* style from Orissa in eastern India. *Patachitra* means painting on canvas – *Pata* is a special canvas made from cloth, and *chitra* means painting. This is the first children's story that uses this beautiful traditional art as book illustration.

The art started around the ancient temple of Puri in Orissa, where artists used to paint the walls with images and stories of the local gods. Visitors to the temple liked to take back a keepsake from their visit, and so artists would create scrolls and cards with traditional stories and tales. These were the first *Patachitras*. Over time, they also made beautiful toys, boxes, games and masks, all painted in the *Patachitra* style.

There are many artists who work in the *Patachitra* style, and they are part of a community. They work together in their homes or in the village square.

Children help their parents and learn the art from them.

When a *Patachitra* artist begins a painting, he first sketches the outlines of his picture. Then the backgrounds and solid colours are painted in, and last of all, the details. Traditionally, artists only used white, yellow, red, black and blue – colours that came from plants and minerals found in the area – but today they use all the different colours available in the market.

Ganjifa Cards

A famous card game painted by *Patachitra* artists is called *Ganjifa*. It uses round handpainted cards, and there are 96 of them in each pack. The rules of the game are very complicated, but we're going to make our own Kanchil *Ganjifa* game, with simple rules.

Kanchil Ganjifa

Cut four cardboard circles, all the same size. On each of them draw Kanchil, Ular, Babi and Harimau on one side. Decorate the borders. Leave the backs of all the cards plain.

This makes one set of cards.

Each player needs two sets of cards. So if you're two players, you need four sets of cards. Or if you're four players, you need eight sets of cards.

Playing the game

The aim is to for the winner to collect all the four characters – the first one to do so wins.

Shuffle the sets of cards and distribute four cards to each player, face down.

Pile the rest of the cards in the centre, face down.

The first player picks a card from the top of the pile. If it's a character she wants, she keeps the card and puts down a card she doesn't want at the bottom of the pile in the centre.

If she's picked a character she doesn't want, she can of course put it away at the bottom of the pile. You should have four cards in your hand at all times. Now it's the turn of the next player, and the game continues until someone has collected all the four characters. That's the winner!

Another Kanchil tale from Nathan Kumar Scott

Monyet the monkey and his friend, Kanchil the mouse deer, plant some trees and look forward to eating the fruit. When they are finally ripe, Monyet climbs up the trees to pick them. But once he gets up there, Monyet can't resist eating all the fruit by himself – and Kanchil can't resist getting even.

A deft and humourous re-telling of one of the best-loved trickster tales in Indonesian folklore, *Mangoes and Bananas* features exquisite art in the traditional Kalamkari style of textile painting from south India.

ISBN 978-81-86211-06-9

Rs.375 | $16.95 | £10.99

"Intense vegetables dyes and stylized flora and fauna provide an unusual backdrop for this amusing folktale." – *Kirkus Reviews*

"The illustrations, done in the traditional Kalamkari style of Indian textile painting, bring a richness to the story... Children will readily relate to the story." – *School Library Journal*

"Well suited to adaptation for student storytelling." – *Booklist*

"Each page is a visual delight... The text is simple, the art exquisite and both capture a tradition of story telling and a centuries-old textile form." – *The Hindu*

For more information visit
www.tarabooks.com
www.nathankumar.com